Postman Pat® and the Spotty Situation

D1122151

SIMON AND SCHUSTER

Jess was snoozing on the Post Office counter while Pat filled his post bag with letters and parcels.

"He's a sleepy boy today," laughed Mrs Goggins.

"Come on, Jess!" chuckled Pat. "We've got work to do!"

Outside the school Pat bumped into Doctor Gilbertson. She was on her way to see the Pottage twins. "They've got a nasty bout of chicken pox."

"Poor things," said Pat. "Let's hope no one else catches it."

When Pat walked into Mr Pringle's classroom, the children were standing at the front, singing away.

Suddenly Sarah Gilbertson gasped. "Look! Lucy's all spotty! And so's Bill! They must have Black River Fever!"

Lucy burst into tears.

"Of course it's not Black River Fever, Sarah!" said Mr Pringle.

"It's probably chicken pox," said Pat. "Tom and Katy have it."

"Dear me!" worried Mr Pringle. "Chicken pox is very infectious!"

By the following day, there were cases of chicken pox all over Greendale.

"Reverend Timms has got it now, and Jeff and Charlie Pringle," Mrs Goggins told Pat.

"And my Julian! He's covered in itchy spots!"

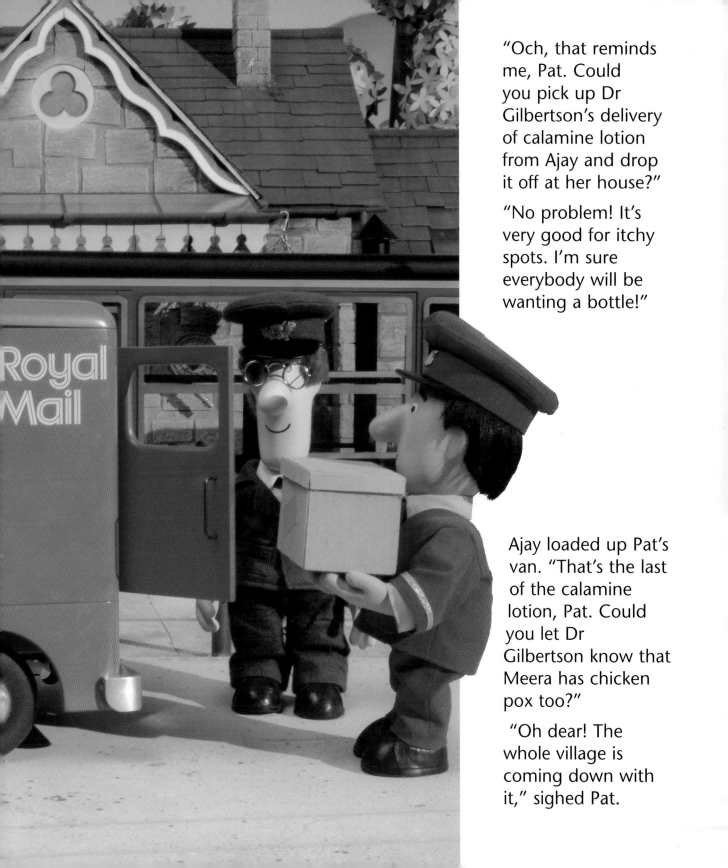

"Och, that reminds me, Pat. Could you pick up Dr Gilbertson's delivery of calamine lotion from Ajay and drop it off at her house?"

"No problem! It's very good for itchy spots. I'm sure everybody will be wanting a bottle!"

Ajay loaded up Pat's van. "That's the last of the calamine lotion, Pat. Could you let Dr Gilbertson know that Meera has chicken pox too?"

"Oh dear! The whole village is coming down with it," sighed Pat.

Pat and Jess made their way to the doctor's house.

Now Sarah was covered in spots!

"Would you mind delivering a bottle of calamine lotion to everyone on this list, Pat?" asked Dr Gilbertson. "I really must keep an eye on Sarah. Oh, and could you take a packet of salt to the vicar?"

Pat was curious. "Why does the vicar want salt?"

"To gargle with, of course!" announced Sarah. "It's very good for sore throats. Tell everyone to put calamine lotion on their spots, and gargle with salt water."

Pat chortled. "Righto, Dr Sarah!"

The vicar was not feeling well at all. He was pleased to get Pat's delivery.

"I'm off to see Jeff and Charlie Pringle now, Reverend – they're poorly too" said Pat.

"Oh Pat! Would you give them something from me? A gardening magazine for Jeff and a comic to cheer up little Charlie?"

"Of course! Oh, and Sarah Gilbertson says, don't forget to gargle!"

Jeff and Charlie were both very spotty. Pat handed Jeff the lotion. "You'll need plenty of this," he said, "and don't forget to gargle!"

Then he gave the comic to Jeff and the gardening magazine to Charlie.

Jess nudged him. "Mia-ow!"

Pat laughed. "Whoops!"
He swapped the comic
and magazine round.
"Well done, Jess!"

Next stop was the Thompsons. Mrs Thompson wondered if Pat could deliver a hot-water bottle to Meera.

The hot-water bottle was shaped like a cat! When Jess saw it, he leapt back in fright. "Mia-ow!"

Pat chuckled. "Don't worry, Jess – it's not real!"

Pat parked outside the Bains'
house. There was a strange
yowling noise coming from
the van. Jess was pouncing
on the hot-water bottle
because he still thought it
was another cat.

"You daft thing, Jess!" laughed Pat as he walked up the path with the last bottle of calamine lotion.

Nisha thought Pat looked worn out.

"It's been a very busy day, and I do have a bit of a sore throat."

"I think you should go home and gargle," said Nisha.

"That's what Sarah Gilbertson says!" Pat said, giving a nasty cough.

Pat was tired out as he drove home. But thanks to him, everyone had soothing calamine lotion for their itchy spots, and the vicar had his gargling salt!

It was dark when Pat and Jess got back.

Julian was much better, but poor Pat was feeling terrible.

It was his turn to be covered in spots!

The next morning, Pat and Jess sat by the fire.
Julian gave Pat a glass of Mrs Goggins' special blackcurrant juice.

"Here you are, Dad. Drink this!"

"Thank you, Julian. You're a very good doctor!"

Julian was well enough to go back to school.

"Are you all better?" asked Mr Pringle.

"I'm fine," said Julian, "but now my dad's got chicken pox!"

"Poor Pat," sighed Mr Pringle. "He spent all day yesterday delivering bottles of calamine lotion and things to make us feel better."

"Mr Pringle, Mr Pringle," cried Sarah, "why don't we do something for Pat?"

Pat and Jess were feeling very sorry for themselves.
Suddenly they heard a noise outside.
Pat opened the front door . . .

. . . and there was the school choir, singing a special song for Pat and Jess!

We want to thank you,
Postman Pat.
We want to thank you
and your black and white cat.
For many years you've been
around,
There's no kinder person
in our town,
Than Pat.
Oh Pat, what would we do
Without YOU?

Jess purred loudly and Pat beamed.

"And what would I do without YOU, Jess?"

SIMON AND SCHUSTER
First published in 2004 in Great Britain by Simon & Schuster UK Ltd
Africa House, 64-78 Kingsway
London WC2B 6AH

A CIP catalogue record for this book is available from the British Library upon request

ISBN 0 689 87250 X

Printed in China

3 5 7 9 10 8 6 4